*✸ Smithsonian

LI on ANGEL ISLAND

BY VEEDA BYBEE
ILLUSTRATED BY ANDREA ROSSETTO

STONE ARCH BOOKS
a capstone imprint

Li on Angel Island is published by Stone Arch Books,
an imprint of Capstone.

1710 Roe Crest Drive
North Mankato, Minnesota 56003
www.capstonepub.com

The name of the Smithsonian Institution and the sunburst logo
are registered trademarks of the Smithsonian Institution. For more
information, please visit www.si.edu.

Library of Congress Cataloging-in-Publication Data is available on
the Library of Congress website.

ISBN: 978-1-4965-9863-9 (hardcover)
ISBN: 978-1-4965-9871-4 (paperback)
ISBN: 978-1-4965-9867-7 (ebook PDF)

Summary: Li, her mother, and her brother journey from China to
America to join their father in San Francisco. But they are detained at
the Angel Island immigration center, where Chinese Americans are
subject to harsh treatment and questioning. Will Li be able to answer
the detailed questions about her former home, and why she wants to
come to America? Or will she fail the tests and be deported?

Designer: Tracy McCabe

Our very special thanks to Megan Smith, Senior Creative Developer,
Officer of Audience Engagement, National Museum of American
History, Smithsonian. Capstone would also like to thank
Kealy Gordon, Product Development Manager, and the following at
Smithsonian Enterprises: Jill Corcoran, Director, Licensed Publishing;
Brigid Ferraro, Vice President, Education and Consumer Products; and
Carol LeBlanc, President, Smithsonian Enterprises.

Printed in the United States of America.
PA117

TABLE OF CONTENTS

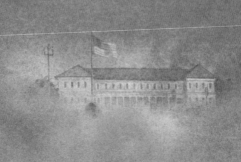

Chapter 1

Land!

November 1921, Angel Island

Li looked over the deck of the *SS San Juan*, the ocean liner she had been traveling on for three weeks. The dark water was gray and choppy, and splashes of cold spray nipped her face.

"Do you see it?" her older brother, Puck, asked as he leaned over the cool metal railings. "Angel Island!" He smiled, not caring that they were getting wet.

Li peered into the distance. The rocky island was surrounded by fog. That made it look as though the sandy shore was the same shade as the sky. It was practically colorless. Already, California looked very different from their home back in China.

"Why is it called Angel Island?" Li asked her brother.

Puck was twelve, and really smart. He knew a lot about everything, especially history. He took a piece of paper out of his pocket and studied the writing. It was a note from Father, and Puck had memorized every word.

"I think Father said it was from the early Spanish explorers. They thought the island protected the water like a guardian angel." Puck quickly looked up. "Do you think we will have to know this fact on the test?"

Li looked down at her feet. Once they landed on Angel Island, all the Chinese passengers would take a test of authenticity. They would have to prove that they were the people listed on their immigration papers.

"I don't think so," Li said. "The test is supposed to see if we are Father's family, not if we know about Angel Island."

Puck played with the folded-up piece of paper. "Do you still have your orange seed?"

Li nodded and showed it to him. Before they'd left their home in Taishan, Puck had suggested Li sneak an orange seed into the seam of one of her shirts. She could plant a little bit of Taishan in their new American home. Puck always had clever ideas.

As the ship sailed closer to shore, Li kept

the orange seed in her hand. "Do you think we will pass the test?"

Leaving their home was hard, but it would have been more difficult to stay. In China, the Fong family had been very poor. Father had been a farmer until he'd left for the United States more than five years ago, when Li was only four years old. His new job as a cook in San Francisco's Chinatown had been a great gift. The U.S. dollar was worth a lot. The money he'd sent back to China gave them food to eat. They could afford rice and clothes.

"I will," Puck said, bumping playfully into Li's shoulder.

"Hey!" Li placed her hands on her hips. Li would miss China and her family and friends there. She would not miss the feeling of being hungry.

Mother had saved up some of the money Father had sent so they could all join Father in San Francisco. He had been gone for so long, Li didn't remember much about him. Li could hardly picture his face. She didn't know how she would prove to the immigration officials that she was his daughter when she didn't even remember what he looked like.

Puck laughed as he teased his sister. "I'll live in America, and you'll be stuck back in China, feeding water buffalo for the rest of your life."

More water splashed onto the ship, sprinkling Li in the face. She wiped the ocean off her cheeks and shook the water onto her brother. "If I go back, who's going to make you something to eat? You always burn the rice."

"Father, of course!" Puck dodged away as Li chased him around the deck. "Maybe I'll get a job in the kitchen with him!"

In the letters Father sent back home, he wrote about his job working as a cook in Chinatown. He said that the restaurant was so popular, even the Americans would come to Chinatown to stand in line to eat his food.

Li laughed. Puck was a terrible cook. "You can't cook," she said. "They will have one bite of your food and kick you out of the country!"

Thinking of food, Li's stomach grumbled. "What do you think we will eat here?"

Puck shrugged. "Anything will be better than the food on this boat."

He started to tear up the paper.

Li watched in shock as her brother threw tiny pieces of paper off the ship. "What are you doing? You need those notes to study."

"I can't let anyone on Angel Island know I had Father's notes." Puck watched the paper sink into the water. "They will think it is proof that we are imposters. Even though we are Father's children, we need to make sure our answers match his."

The boat rocked, and Li felt dizzy. "I haven't seen Father in so long. How can I convince people when I don't remember him very well?"

Just then, Mother came up to them. She had been in their quarters, collecting the few belongings they had. "You don't have to remember Father to know he loves you."

Li leaned against her mother. "It feels so strange to leave China. I don't know where I belong."

Mother placed her arms around Li. "You are still from China. You will also be from America. You are no different from the rest of the people who come to the United States, each with one foot in their past and the other in the present."

Puck looked over the water. "I can't wait to put both feet on the ground again."

Soon the fog parted, and the ship reached the shore. People started to leave. Puck and Li stayed close to Mother as they made their way onto Angel Island.

Once everyone was off the ship, men in uniforms looked over the passengers. They were sorted into groups: the Japanese, then other Asians, and, last, the Chinese.

Li noticed that the white passengers walked right into the buildings on Angel Island. They didn't have to wait to be counted or placed in a group.

"Why don't they have to wait?" Li asked Mother.

Mother looked out into the ocean. "They aren't Chinese."

Suddenly, there was a guard next to them. He was speaking loudly. Li felt her head spin. English sounded so fast. Someone translated the guard's English words into Chinese.

"How old is your son?" the translator asked Mother.

"Twelve," Mother answered.

The translator spoke to the guard. The guard nodded and motioned for Puck to follow him.

"What is happening?" Mother's voice was frantic.

"Children under twelve remain with their mothers. Your son is older and will be placed with the men on Angel Island," the translator said.

Puck, who usually seemed so strong, looked scared.

"I'll keep an eye on him," a man in the group offered. He was a friend they'd made on the ship. "Puck will be safe with me."

Mother still looked anxious, but she tried to smile. "Thank you."

Li could not hide her worry. Her brother would not be with her. "No! Puck!" Li called out. She ran toward the group of men.

"Li!" Mother said.

Li pushed past the guards. She held Puck tightly. Hugging her brother felt like they were still back home, where no one could separate them.

A guard walked over to Li. He spoke English in a loud voice. He was gruff and sounded angry though she couldn't understand what he said. Grabbing her arm, he pushed her away from Puck.

Li stumbled and fell to the ground. She held out her hands to catch her fall. As she did, the orange seed she had been holding tumbled to the earth.

"No!" Li said.

She looked around in the dirt, but it was no use. The orange seed was lost.

Chapter 2

First Test

Li shuffled her feet in line. Mother tried to whisper comforting things, but Li couldn't listen. She could hardly hear all the translated instructions from the guards. Puck was gone. Father was far away. She had lost her orange seed—the only bit of home she had left.

The group of women and children were led into a room. They were given crackers and bread that were stale and dry. Li wished for something hot, like rice porridge topped with vegetables and chicken.

"Time for the medical inspection!" the translator said. The translator explained to them that they were in a detention center, a building where they would be examined for health before entering the main center on Angel Island. If they were not healthy, they could be sent back to China or spend the first few weeks in the hospital getting well. All the women and children lined up in single file.

This was their first test on Angel Island.

Immediately, Li was worried. She tugged on her mother's sleeve and remembered her brother. "Puck has been sick," she said. "Will he be sent back?"

Mother smiled, but her forehead wrinkled in worry. "He was feeling better.

I'm sure your brother will be okay."

The long line had still barely moved. It was as slow as a plow in the rice fields. As Li stared ahead, she imagined riding a water buffalo through Angel Island. The water buffalo would crash through the stone walls, and Li would rescue her brother. Together, they would collect Mother. Somehow, they would swim across the bay to San Francisco and be reunited with Father.

As Li waited for the medical inspection, she noticed a boy standing nearby. He seemed to be about her age. It looked like he had no family with him. The boy wiped tears from his face.

Li thought of Puck, who might be feeling the same way as this boy. She didn't want anyone feeling like they were alone.

She tapped the boy on the shoulder. "Hello. I'm Fong Li," she said, using the formal last name first. What's your name?"

He sniffed. "Wang Hon."

Hon was shaking. He looked like he could use a big bowl of hot food or a warm blanket.

Li had nothing to give him but a smile. So she did.

"Where are you from?" Li asked.

Hon looked at Li's face and seemed to warm up. "Right now, nowhere. Where I used to live isn't what I'm supposed to tell anyone." He dropped his voice and leaned closer to Li. "I am pretending to be my uncle's son. He sent papers over for me so I can live with him in America."

Li nodded. "You're a paper son."

Many of the Chinese were having their children come to America as paper sons and daughters or documented legal children of others. They were often extended family members who were trying to give children a better life with more opportunities.

Immigration for the Chinese was very tough. There were many rules in place to prevent them from coming to America. In his letters back home, Father wrote about the hatred many people in America felt toward immigrants from China. They thought they were taking away jobs from people who had been born in the United States.

Father said there were many laws to stop Chinese people from moving to America. It seemed like the rules were getting stricter every day. That's why Father thought it best for Li's family to come to America now, before even more restrictions were added.

Hon looked at the ground. "I'm not in China, I'm not in America. I am no one."

He looked so lost. Li felt sorry for him. Even though her first day on Angel Island was sad, at least she had Mother with her. Even if Puck was separated from them, she knew he was still on the island.

Li knew Hon did not have his mother with him. She thought of her own and met Hon's eye.

"You are still from China," she said, repeating Mother's words. "You will also be from America. You are no different from the rest of us, each with one foot in our past and the other in our present." Li gestured around the room. "We all came here for a better life."

Hon looked down at his hands. "I'm so afraid I'm going to fail the test. I will be

sent home, and all the money my family saved up will go to waste."

Li thought of Puck. She remembered how much he had helped her study. Puck would want Li to help others too.

Li smiled at Hon. This time, she hoped it shone even brighter. "I will help you. We will get off Angel Island together."

Hon glanced up at Li. He looked hopeful. "Thank you," he said.

Just then, Li noticed they were at the front of the line. She was startled to see the workers at the hospital dressed all in white. It was frightening. White was the color of funerals in China. Li felt like she was walking toward her own death.

"Once you are behind the curtain," a translator said, "remove all your clothing for the examination."

Li looked for Mother, but she had been moved into another line across the room.

Li felt scared. She had never been inspected like this before. Maybe this was the end for her. She couldn't study or prepare for a medical test. Either she was healthy, or she wasn't.

When it was time for her inspection, Li didn't look at anyone. She was embarrassed to stand in front of strangers without any clothes on.

After her examination, Li was found healthy. She had passed the first test. She hoped that Puck had passed too.

Li rejoined mother. Mother had passed the test too. Without speaking, they embraced.

Li was still worried. This first test, without any words, had been hard.

How am I going to pass the exam where I have to answer questions, Li wondered? In her first hours on Angel Island, she had already been sorted into a group. Separated from her brother. Looked over for physical health.

Li was starting to feel less like a person and more like an animal being herded around. This feeling almost made Li forget why she was here and where she really came from. Would she be able to hold on to her memories of China and remember who she was?

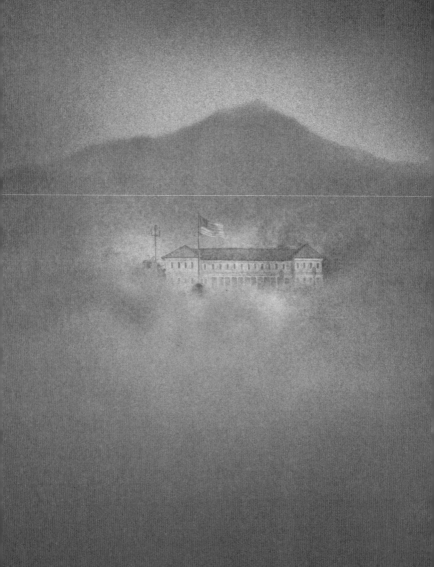

Chapter 3

Oranges

Li and Mother followed the rest of the group of women and children to their barracks—the building where they would live. With help from an interpreter, Angel Island guards showed them around and explained that there were separate buildings for the Chinese immigrants. The women and children were kept apart from the men, and all Chinese people were segregated from the white immigrants.

There was a dining hall for the Chinese where the men and women would eat in shifts to avoid seeing one another. The women had their own outside play area, and their own barracks.

The guards showed them their living quarters on Angel Island. Bunk beds stacked two or three high were crammed into a large room. Bare light bulbs hung from the ceiling. A ping-pong table was at the end of the room. The windows had iron bars on them.

On the wall, Li saw markings. She looked closer and saw that they were words.

"Mother," Li said. "Look."

Mother squeezed Li's hand tight. "So many sorrowful stories on these walls."

Li looked around. Poems were scrawled out in several places. Li was glad that there

32

was no poetry near her bunk. She didn't want to sleep underneath such sadness.

Li sank onto her bed. This was her home for now. If she didn't pass the test, it might be her only home in America. It didn't feel like a home, though. She glanced at the poetry on the walls. It was more like a prison.

Mother stood next to her at the window and pointed out San Francisco to the west as well as Oakland to the east. Then she pointed across the window.

"Father is there," Mother said. "Just across those waters. We will be reunited with him soon."

Li continued to look out the barred windows onto the bay. All she saw was the dark water keeping them from entering San Francisco. She hoped Mother was right.

That evening, Li went outside to play and study with Hon. They talked about village life back home. They shared the same love of water buffalo and oranges.

Li leaned in close to Hon. "I brought an orange seed from back home," she said.

Hon frowned. "Why?"

"I was planning on growing an orange tree in my new home." Li looked around the island. "Except I dropped it in the dirt."

Hon kicked around a rock. "Well, Angel Island is your home. Maybe it will take root here and grow."

"Hopefully it's on the Chinese side of the island," Li said.

There were two courtyards on Angel Island. Like the dining hall, they were segregated. One was for the white immigrants and the other was for the

Chinese. Li did not like the division.

Hon peered out over the fence that separated them. "If everyone else is nice, maybe we will share our oranges."

"If we had our water buffalo," Li said, "I would ride through the courtyard and tear down this fence between us."

Li and Hon laughed. Then Li heard a woman on the Chinese side of the courtyard crying.

A couple of women near Li started to whisper. "She did not pass the test," one woman said.

"How sad," the other woman answered. "Now she will have to go back."

It felt like a sack of oranges had hit Li in the stomach. She thought of the sad poetry on the walls of the barracks. The test was real. If she didn't pass the next test, she

would go back to China on the next boat—
without Mother, Puck, or Father. She would
be just like this woman in the courtyard.
Separated from her family and all alone.

****

December 1921, Angel Island

A month passed, and Li and Mother
settled into their new life on Angel Island.
Since the women and children were
separated from the men, they did not
see Puck. Every day Li thought about her
brother as she waited for her turn to be
questioned. The exam could take days
or even longer. Mother had already gone
through three days of questioning. She
hoped it would be over soon.

Li tried to remember the answers she
had studied. If Mother hadn't told her that

it had only been a month since they arrived on Angel Island, Li would have thought they had been there for years. She was starting to forget her life back in China. The water buffalo and orange trees were beginning to feel like a dream.

One afternoon, Hon met Li at their usual spot in the courtyard. She was bouncing a ball between her hands when he came up to her. He looked pale.

"I had more questions today," he said.

Li stopped dribbling and held the ball. Hon had been in questioning all week. "How did it go?"

Hon couldn't look at her. "I was so nervous. I grew up in the same village as my uncle, so I know everything about it. But they asked me where we keep the rice bin in the house, and I didn't know.

I'd visited my uncle, but I never prepared the rice."

He finally looked at Li. "I have to go back for questioning tomorrow."

Li took his hand in hers. "Then you still have time. I think it's almost dinner. Let's go together."

Every day, Li looked forward to going to the Chinese dining hall on Angel Island. Not because the food tasted good—Li thought it was actually very bland and soupy. The workers tried to make food from China. The cooks were even Chinese. But the food they made wasn't anything like what Li used to eat at home. Mother said it was because the cooks didn't have the proper equipment.

Li liked going to eat because, during mealtime, the women and children could hear the footsteps of the men coming up the stairs. It was one of the only ways they could communicate with their separated family members. As they walked up, the men called out to their families, sometimes with a quick greeting of love or with a coded message.

This was how Mother and Li learned that Puck was okay. The day before, Puck had passed them a message that he had started his test. It had lasted all day, and he didn't know when it would all be over.

Today, Li poked around at her plate of food. There wasn't a good crispy fry on the rice. It was just as mushy and soupy as the rest of her food.

Li laughed as Hon licked up his last grain of rice. "You must be really hungry," she joked.

Hon looked up from his plate. "Sometimes at home, we had to eat grass because there was nothing to eat. I'll take this over weeds any day." He paused. "It's why my mother spent all our savings for me to come to America. This food is better than no food at all."

Li thought about what Hon was doing for a better life. She knew he would also work and send money back home to his family once he got to the mainland. He was risking everything just to put food on the table.

Li placed her spoon down. "You will pass the test, Hon. Let's practice some more."

Just then, they heard the steady stomping of feet. The men were walking by the dining hall!

Li quickly got up. She pretended to throw something away and stood near the door so she could hear better.

The rumble of deep voices filled the air. Li listened for Puck's voice. She worried that she wouldn't hear it. Maybe his test had gone badly yesterday. He could be on a ship headed back to China right now!

Then Li heard a familiar laugh. She could recognize this voice across an island. Puck was here. Li felt relief that her brother was still being questioned and had not been sent back.

"Don't forget the oranges!" Puck said.

Li leaned closer to hear more, but there was no other message.

Oranges? she thought as the steps faded away. *What is the importance of oranges?*

Chapter 4

Hon

The next day, Li went to find Hon.
She wanted to ask his thoughts on Puck's
message. But Hon wasn't at breakfast. By
dinner time, Li still hadn't seen him. She
walked over to the dining hall alone.

The dinner hour started, and Hon never
came. Sitting next to Mother, Li ate her
mushy rice and vegetables in silence. An
uneasiness washed over her. It wasn't like
Hon to miss out on food.

After dinner, Li walked quickly to the courtyard. Maybe Hon was waiting for her outside. She entered the Chinese courtyard area and made it to their spot on the field.

There was no one waiting for her. Hon was nowhere to be seen.

Li headed back to the barracks. She had to keep herself from running. When she got to Hon's bunk, she gasped. It no longer looked like Hon's bed. The bedding was stripped down, and there was no sign of his belongings.

Li asked around, but no one knew what had happened to Hon.

Li walked slowly back down to the courtyard. She bounced a ball around. Each thump against the pavement sounded hollow and empty.

Maybe Hon had passed his test, she thought.

It was possible his uncle had picked him up from Angel Island. Li hoped that was true, but a sinking feeling settled in her stomach. It was also possible that Hon hadn't passed the test. He might have been sent back to China.

Li drew circles in the dirt with her fingers. What had happened to her friend?

Just then, an older Chinese woman came up to Li. She glanced around the courtyard, then huddled close to Li. "Are you Fong Li?"

"Yes." Li spoke quietly.

The woman pulled out an orange from the folds of her shirt. She dropped the fruit into Li's hands. "This is from your brother. What is inside is the sweetest reward."

Li quickly placed the orange in her pocket and bowed her head in thanks. She hurried to her barracks. The orange felt like it was burning a hole through her clothing.

In the safety of her top bunk, Li turned toward the light of the window and held the orange in her hands. She ran her fingers over the smooth skin. And she realized the top of the orange was cut out like a lid.

Li nudged her fingers under the orange lid. The orange was hollowed out, with a tiny roll of paper tucked inside. Puck had given her a secret message.

Li could barely breathe. She slowly unfolded the note. In her brother's handwriting were notes about Taishan. It included the families that lived around them, the layout of the town, and details about where the Fong family home was—all things that Li might have forgotten.

Li looked out the barred window. Even if Puck was in a separate area of Angel Island, right then, he felt close by. He had taken the test and made sure to help his sister.

Before she went to sleep, Li showed Mother the note.

Mother smiled as she read over the message. "Puck is very smart to communicate this way."

Li held her Mother close and thought about her brother. Puck always had clever ideas.

Mother handed the paper back to Li. "I know all these details. Please memorize them for yourself, and then destroy the note. Your brother went through all this trouble for you, and we don't want him to get caught."

As Li nodded off to sleep, she thought of oranges, her brave brother, and her missing friend. She was determined to memorize every word of Puck's note. Otherwise, she might disappear like Hon.

Chapter 5

Questions

The time for Li's examination came sooner than she thought. The next morning, she was called for the test to prove her identity. She quickly read over Puck's paper again. Li was grateful for the time she'd had to study last night.

Before she left for her test, Mother pulled Li in for a hug and said, "May our ancestors be with you."

Li followed others who were being questioned and stood in a long line. Some people looked very confident. Others seemed to be nervous. Li was somewhere in between.

After what seemed like hours, it was her turn for questioning. When she entered the room, Li saw four people. Two seated white men and a Chinese woman standing behind them. There was also a woman at a typewriter. Li knew the woman was there to record Li's answers.

One of the white men held a pen in his hand and wrote in a notebook.

He must be the main interrogator, Li thought.

The Chinese woman stood to the man's right. She spoke to Li and said she would be the interpreter for her test.

All the adults looked at Li. Suddenly, she felt very small. She wished Mother was with her, but parents and children were questioned separately. The officials didn't want the Chinese adults to help any of the children.

The interrogator pushed up his glasses. "Fong Li," he said as the Chinese interpreter translated. "Shall we begin?"

Li could not find words to come out of her mouth. She nodded quickly.

The man shuffled his papers and read the first question. "What are the names of the people in your family?"

Li swallowed. She forced her mouth to speak. She answered in Chinese. "Fong Tom is my father. Fong Shee, my mother." When she thought about Puck, her voice grew stronger. "Fong Puck is my older brother."

The questions continued.

"Who is the oldest person in your village?"

"What is your father's profession?"

"Is your house one story or two stories?"

These questions went on for more than an hour.

Li's head hurt. Trying to remember details about her life was tiring. She tried to separate what she could recall from her own memory from the things she had studied on the paper her brother had sent her in the orange.

Eventually, Li was taken into the hallway for a break. Minutes later, she was called back again.

The exam lasted into the afternoon. When Li came back into the room after another break, there was a set of wooden blocks on the table.

The white man with the notebook spoke. "Recreate your village using these blocks," the interpreter translated.

Li froze. It had been so long since she'd been in China. And talking to these adults made her nervous. She stared at the blocks and tried to picture them looking like the buildings back home. It was no use. They just looked like blocks.

She thought of her brother doing this same test. Li wondered how Puck had arranged the blocks. She remembered Puck's words in the dining hall: *Don't forget the oranges!*

Li looked up. That was the key! Puck knew Li would not forget about the oranges. If she could remember where the orange tree was in the family farm, Li could center the village around the tree.

Li closed her eyes for a moment. In her memory, she could see the water buffalo in the fields. She saw the dirt path leading up to the front door of her old house. Just to the right of the house was the orange tree. Sunlight poured down on the tree, shining on the bright green leaves. Big clusters of bright orange fruit hung heavy from the branches.

Seeing the tree so clearly in her mind, Li felt like she was home. There was her grandparents' house. She could see the neighbors and the market.

Li opened her eyes.

She remembered where she came from.

Li took the wooden blocks in her hand and arranged them on the table. "Here is my home," she said. "This is where the orange tree is."

She laid the other pieces out quickly. This part of the test was like a game—one she knew she could win. For the first time, Li felt confidence flow through her as she completed the layout of her village.

The adults took notes. Li heard the clicking of the typewriter. She knew that whatever they wrote up, her memory was true. She was a Chinese daughter. Sister of Puck. The orange tree clue painted a picture of her home in China. It helped her remember where she was from.

After creating her village from blocks, the questions were fewer. The interrogator seemed satisfied. Li was finally free to go.

Walking out of the room, Li felt much different from when she'd entered. For the first time since arriving on Angel Island, dread did not weigh on her. She'd answered the questions as truthfully as she could. Whatever the outcome would be, she'd tried her best.

Back in the dormitory, Li waited for Mother. A guard would let them know if they would be leaving Angel Island on a boat to San Francisco, or back to China.

Mother came in. She had been taking her own exam. Mother looked tired, but also hopeful.

"How was the test?" Mother said.

"I remembered who I am," Li said.

"That is all we can do." Mom held out her hands. "I have good news. I heard from one of the interpreters that Puck passed the exam. Father will soon pick him up."

Li threw her arms around Mother. Just then, a guard opened the door. He wore a happy face. He pointed to Li and Mother.

"Good fortune!" he called. "Go ashore!"

Li smiled so hard it warmed her all over. "We passed too!"

She hugged Mother as everyone in the room cheered.

She was a proud Chinese girl, both feet pointed toward her new life in America.

THE HISTORY BEHIND ANGEL ISLAND

Located in the San Francisco Bay just about five miles north of San Francisco, Angel Island served as the United States immigration station for the West Coast for thirty years. From 1910 to 1940, it was the first stop for many coming to America.

During this time, many people left their home country to seek a new life, Chinese immigrants included. With a poor rural economy in China and many natural disasters, they looked to opportunities in the United States for better jobs. The Chinese immigrants became an important part of building the American West, working in mining, railroad, agricultural, and other jobs.

Of the almost one million people who came through Angel Island, 175,000 were Chinese. With harsh laws such as the Chinese Exclusion Act, which was put into place in 1882 to prohibit immigrants from China, it was difficult to come to America. This was the first time the United States restricted immigration based on race. Hatred and racism against the Chinese immigrants was very high. They were paid lower wages than white workers in the same jobs, and were then blamed for driving down pay and taking away jobs.

The Chinese Exclusion Act was repealed in 1943, but immigration was still very limited. From 1943 until 1965, only 105 Chinese immigrants were allowed each year.

The immigration station on Angel Island was built in 1910 in order to enforce the Chinese Exclusion Act. This location was selected because it was an island. It separated immigrants from friends and family on the mainland.

The average stay on Angel Island was two weeks for Chinese immigrants. Some were detained even longer, from several months to almost two years.

The immigration station could handle 2,500 immigrants a day with sleeping accommodations for 1,000. The Chinese were forced to stay in crowded barracks. Sometimes as many as 200 people were packed into a room meant to hold fifty.

Under the Chinese Exclusion Act, more Chinese men could enter the United States than women. On average, Angel Island held around 200 to 300 men, and thirty to fifty women.

Early on, the Chinese American community complained about the unsanitary and hazardous conditions on Angel Island. In 1940, a fire burned down the administration building, ending the immigration station on Angel Island. The remaining immigrants were sent to different locations in the San Francisco Bay.

Life on Angel Island was tough for the Chinese immigrants. Many people expressed frustration by carving poetry into the walls.

In these poems, they wrote of the harsh conditions on Angel Island. Of the fear, sadness, and loneliness they felt.

> *Lim, upon arriving in America,*
> *Was arrested, put in the wooden building,*
> *And made a prisoner.*

These poems were found in 1970 when a park ranger came across them in a building that was about to be torn down. Some poems have been saved and are on display today in the Angel Island Detention Barracks. Visitors can see the words carved on the walls about the hardships of those who faced the tests on Angel Island.

ORANGE CAKE SURPRISE

Like the orange Puck gave to Li, this orange has a sweet surprise in the center.

Supplies

- aluminum foil
- baking sheet
- sharp knife
- 10 large oranges
- 1 box of yellow or vanilla cake mix
- 3 large eggs
- ⅓ cup canola oil

Directions

Preheat oven to 350 degrees. With help from an adult, create a lid from each orange by slicing off the top quarter. Using a large spoon, remove the fruit from the top and inside the orange. This will create an empty orange peel. Repeat this step for all oranges. Using a juicer if you have one, or your hands if you don't, squeeze one cup of juice from the oranges. Set aside the remaining fruit to make more orange juice or save for another use.

In a large bowl, combine the cake mix, eggs, oil, and orange juice. Mix until smooth. Then spoon the cake batter into each empty orange, until about two-thirds full. Place the orange lid on top and wrap each fruit completely in aluminum foil. Place the filled oranges on a cookie sheet with the tops facing up. Bake for about 20–25 minutes.

Ask an adult to remove the orange cakes from the oven. Let cool for 5–10 minutes. Once cooled, peel away the foil. Remove the tops and enjoy.

GLOSSARY

ancestor (AN-sess-tuhr)—member of a person's family who lived a long time ago

authenticity (aw-then-TI-sih-tee)—the nature of being real or genuine

barracks (BAR-uhks)—a large, plain building or group of buildings where many people live

immigrant (IM-uh-gruhnt)—a person who leaves one country to settle in another

imposter (IM-pos-tuhr)—a person who pretends to be someone else.

inspection (in-SPEK-shuhn)—the process of looking over or reviewing something

interpreter (in-TUR-pri-tuhr)—a person who can tell others what is said in another language

interrogator (in-TEHR-uh-gay-tuhr)—a person who questions thoroughly, often for official reasons

paper son (PAY-puhr SUN)—a child from China who tried to immigrate to the United States using fake documents

passenger (PASS-ehn-juhr)—a person who travels by car, ship, train, or other public or private vehicles, and is not the driver or a crewmember

restriction (ri-STRICK-shuhn)—a rule or limitation

segregated (SEHG-reh-gay-ted)—separated by race

ABOUT THE AUTHOR

A former journalist, Veeda Bybee holds a master's in fine arts from the Vermont College of the Arts. She is the daughter of Asian immigrants and lives in Nevada with her family.

ABOUT THE ILLUSTRATOR

Andrea Rossetto was born in 1977 in Italy. Drawing has always been his greatest passion! He has worked as an illustrator since 2004 with companies including Disney, Cambridge University Press, Les Humanoides Associes, Soleil Editions, and Bamboo. He teaches drawing and digital coloring at the International School of Comics in Padua. He has a wife and a son whom he loves a lot, and a box full of dreams!